nickelodeon

DORA the EXPLORER

DORA'S BIG BIRTHDAY ADVENTURE

Adapted by Lauryn Silverhardt
Based on the screenplay by Valerie Walsh Valdes
Illustrated by Robert Roper

A Random House PICTUREBACK® Book
Random House 🏠 New York

randomhouse.com/kids
ISBN: 978-0-449-81445-1
Printed in the United States of America
10 9 8 7 6 5

¡Hola, soy Dora! Boots and I are in the Magic Storybook, where we have been on lots of exciting adventures, but now we are ready to go home. Do you know why? Because today is my birthday!

Do you like birthday parties? Me too! My friends and family are having a birthday party for me! Will you come to my birthday party? *¡Fantástico!* I can't wait to go back home for the party!

Oh, no! A twisty wind cloud is carrying us away. It looks like we are headed to another part of the Magic Storybook! Hold on, Boots!

The twisty wind cloud blew us all the way to Wizzle World. But that's okay. All we have to do is jump out of the Magic Storybook and we'll be back in the rainforest in no time. Ready? Let's jump!

Hmm. Jumping out of the storybook isn't working. Boots and I are still in Wizzle World. The Wizzles want to help us. They remember Boots and me because we helped them before. The Wizzles tell us that the only way to get home from Wizzle World is if the Wishing Wizzle wishes us home. But the Wishing Wizzle can't make any more wishes because he doesn't have his wishing crystal!

¡Mira! I have a crystal! The Wizzles tell me that this is the wishing crystal. Now we just need to get it to the Wishing Wizzle so he can wish us back to the rainforest! *¡Vámonos!* Let's go!

The Wizzles warn us to be careful of La Bruja, the Mean Witch. She doesn't like wishes. She's the one who took the Wishing Wizzle's wishing crystal so he couldn't make any more wishes.

We're off to see the Wishing Wizzle! But where is he? Who do we ask for help when we don't know which way to go? Yeah, Map!

Map says to get to the Wishing Wizzle, we go across the Sea Snake Lake, then through the Dancing Forest, and then over the Rainbow. Then we'll reach the Wishing Wizzle, and he can wish us back home for my birthday party!

We made it to Sea Snake Lake, and I see a big, big snake! How will we get across the lake? I know—that bubble can carry us across the lake above the sea snake!

Look! It's La Bruja, the Mean Witch. She's zapping our bubble and popping holes in it! This is not good!

My crystal is lighting up—the Snow Princess has a message for us. She says we'll need the help of our friends to get past La Bruja. If we need help, we can ask the crystal to remember our friends. Say *"¡Recuerda a mis amigos!"*

The crystal shows us a time when Benny had a hole in his hot-air balloon. Remember how we brought Benny sticky tape to fix his balloon? We can also use sticky tape to patch up the holes in the bubble. I have some sticky tape in my Backpack. Say "Backpack!"

Do you see the sticky tape? Smart looking!

We have to tape up the holes quickly. But first we need to count the holes. Count with me! 1, 2, 3, 4, 5, 6, 7, 8, 9, 10, 11. Eleven holes.

Good counting! Now let's tape them up.

Yay! We made it past Sea Snake Lake. So next is the Dancing Forest. But first we need to go through this field of flowers.

Look! One of the flowers has Boots's tail! We need to help Boots. The snappy flowers speak Spanish, so we need to help Boots say "open" in Spanish. Say *"¡Abre, por favor!"* Open, please!

You did it! Thanks for helping Boots!

We're at the entrance to the Dancing Forest, but the trees aren't dancing. La Bruja put a spell on the trees that made them stop dancing— and now they're trying to stop us from getting through the forest!

We need to ask the crystal to remember our friends! Say *"¡Recuerda a mis amigos!"* Remember how we helped the Pirate Piggies dance past the Coconut Conga trees? I bet if we danced the Coconut Conga, the trees will want to dance and they'll have to let us go through. Let's wiggle, wiggle, wiggle!

Great job! We made it through the Dancing Forest. Where do we go next? The Rainbow! Yeah! *El arco iris*. Thanks for helping. We just need to follow this path to the Rainbow. Let's go!

Uh-oh. The path stopped. How are we going to get to the Rainbow? Maybe that scarecrow knows the way.

The scarecrow is crying. He says that the crows keep scaring him, even though it's his job to scare the crows away. The scarecrow says he will lead us to the Rainbow if we can show him how to scare the crows away. That's easy. To scare crows away, all you have to say is "Boo!" Say it with us: "Boo!"

We did it! Good job!

The scarecrow points us in the direction of the Rainbow.
Thanks, scarecrow! We have to travel over the Rainbow to get to
the Wishing Wizzle. Do you see someone who can take us there?
A unicorn! Smart looking!

Oh, no! La Bruja made it rain, and the Rainbow is disappearing! We need help—and fast. Tell the crystal *"¡Recuerda a mis amigos!"* Remember our friends! Look at the crystal! Our friends are singing, *"Rain, rain, go away! Come again another day!"* Sing with us!

It's working! The Rainbow is coming back!

We made it over the Rainbow. *¡Gracias, Unicornio!* And there's the Wishing Wizzle. He's so happy to see that we brought him his crystal—now he can grant wishes again! And he can wish us home for my birthday!

Oh, no! La Bruja has cracked the crystal with her bolts of lightning. The Wishing Wizzle says that the wishing crystal has lost its power, but there might be one way to make it work again. The Wishing Wizzle says I will need all of my friends to help. Everyone has to wish really hard. They have to say "I wish Dora back home."

Our friends are wishing us home! But the Wishing Wizzle says the crystal needs more power. There's just one friend who's missing—it's you! Will you wish us back home? Say "I wish Dora back home!"

It worked! We made it home for my party! We couldn't have done it without help from our friends—and you! Thank you for helping Boots and me get back home for my party. This is the best birthday ever!